W9-BMW-388

Copyright © 2014 Disney Enterprises, Inc., and Pixar Animation Studios. All rights reserved. Published by Disney Press, an imprint of Disney Book Group. No part of this book may be reproduced or transmitted in any form or by any means, electronic or mechanical, including photocopying, recording, or by any information storage and retrieval system, without written permission from the publisher.
For information address Disney Press, 1101 Flower Street, Glendale, California 91201.

This special edition was printed for Kohl's Department Stores, Inc. (for distribution on behalf of Kohl's Cares, LLC, its wholly owned subsidiary), by Disney Press, New York/Los Angeles.

Kohl's
1224426-00
123387
09/14–10/14

Printed in China
First Edition
1 3 5 7 9 10 8 6 4 2
ISBN 978-1-4847-2384-5 • G615-7693-2-14286

For more Disney Press fun, visit www.disneybooks.com

Disney PRESS
New York • Los Angeles

"Hey, Woody! Ready to go to cowboy camp?" Andy shouted, bursting into his bedroom.

Woody was a cowboy doll. He was one of Andy's favorite toys. His other favorite was a space ranger named Buzz.

"Never tangle with the unstoppable duo of Woody and Buzz Lightyear," Andy cried, linking the toys' arms together.

Suddenly, there was a loud *RIIIP*.

Woody's shoulder had ripped open!

Andy's mom suggested fixing Woody on the way to camp, but Andy shook his head. "No, just leave him," he said.

Andy handed the cowboy to his mom, who put the doll on a shelf. Sheriff Woody wouldn't be going to cowboy camp after all.

A few days later, Andy's mom began to clean his room. She was having a yard sale and wanted to get rid of Andy's old toys.

Andy's mom grabbed Wheezy the penguin and brought him into the yard. Woody couldn't let her give his friend away!

Woody whistled for Andy's dog, Buster. He climbed onto Buster's back, and the two raced outside to save the penguin.

But Woody couldn't hold on with a broken arm. He fell off Buster and was picked up by a strange man.

The man's name was Al. When no one was looking, he hid Woody in his coat. Then he hopped in his car and drove away. The other toys watched from the window. They had to save Woody!

Al took Woody to his apartment. Suddenly, a packing crate burst open. Out popped a cowgirl named Jessie and a toy horse named Bullseye.

"Yee-haw! It's really you!" Jessie shouted.

Woody was confused. Why were the toys so happy to see him?

"Let's show him who he really is!" said an old prospector doll named Pete.

Jessie turned on an old TV show called *Woody's Roundup*. Woody could hardly believe his eyes. He was the star!

Prospector Pete explained that the Roundup toys had become valuable collectibles. Now that Al had a Woody doll, he was selling the whole set to a museum . . . in Japan!

Meanwhile, back at Andy's house, Buzz had figured out that Al was the owner of the local toy store. The toys set out at once to rescue their friend.

As the sun rose, they spotted Al's Toy Barn. It was on the other side of a busy road. The toys each picked up a traffic cone and dashed across the street.

Inside the Toy Barn, Buzz found an amazing display of new Buzz Lightyear toys. Each one was wearing a super utility pack.

As Buzz reached for the utility pack, a hand grabbed his wrist. It was a new Buzz Lightyear toy. The toy thought he had caught a rogue space ranger. He quickly tied Buzz to a box and placed him back on the shelf. Then the new Buzz ran off to join Andy's toys.

Meanwhile, the other toys had found Al's office. Listening to him on the phone, they realized that Al planned to sell Woody!

As the toys climbed into Al's briefcase, Buzz broke free. He followed his friends. But Buzz was being followed, too . . . by the evil Emperor Zurg!

Not far away, Woody's arm had been repaired. He looked brand-new. He was ready to go home to Andy.

"I belonged to a little girl once," said Jessie sadly. "She played with me every day, until she grew up. Then she gave me away. Even the greatest kids outgrow their toys."

Woody began to worry that Andy would forget about him, too. Maybe it was better to go to the museum.

Meanwhile, the new Buzz and Andy's toys had arrived at Al's apartment building. The new Buzz pulled the grate off an air vent for the toys to crawl through. "Come on," he said. "We've got no time to lose."

When the toys reached the apartment, they were excited to see Woody. New Buzz grabbed Woody. Slinky wrapped Jessie and Bullseye up in his coils, and Hamm jumped on the Prospector's box.

"Hold it right there!" a voice said suddenly. It was the real Buzz!

"There's no time to explain. Come on, Woody! Let's go," the real Buzz said. But to his amazement, Woody refused. What if his shoulder broke again? Would Andy still want him?

As the toys turned to leave, Woody watched a small, smiling boy on the TV. It made him realize how much he missed Andy.

"Hey, Buzz! Wait!" he shouted. He started to follow his friends, but the Prospector blocked the way. He had spent his whole life in a box, and he was ready for the museum.

At that moment, the toys heard footsteps. Al was coming!

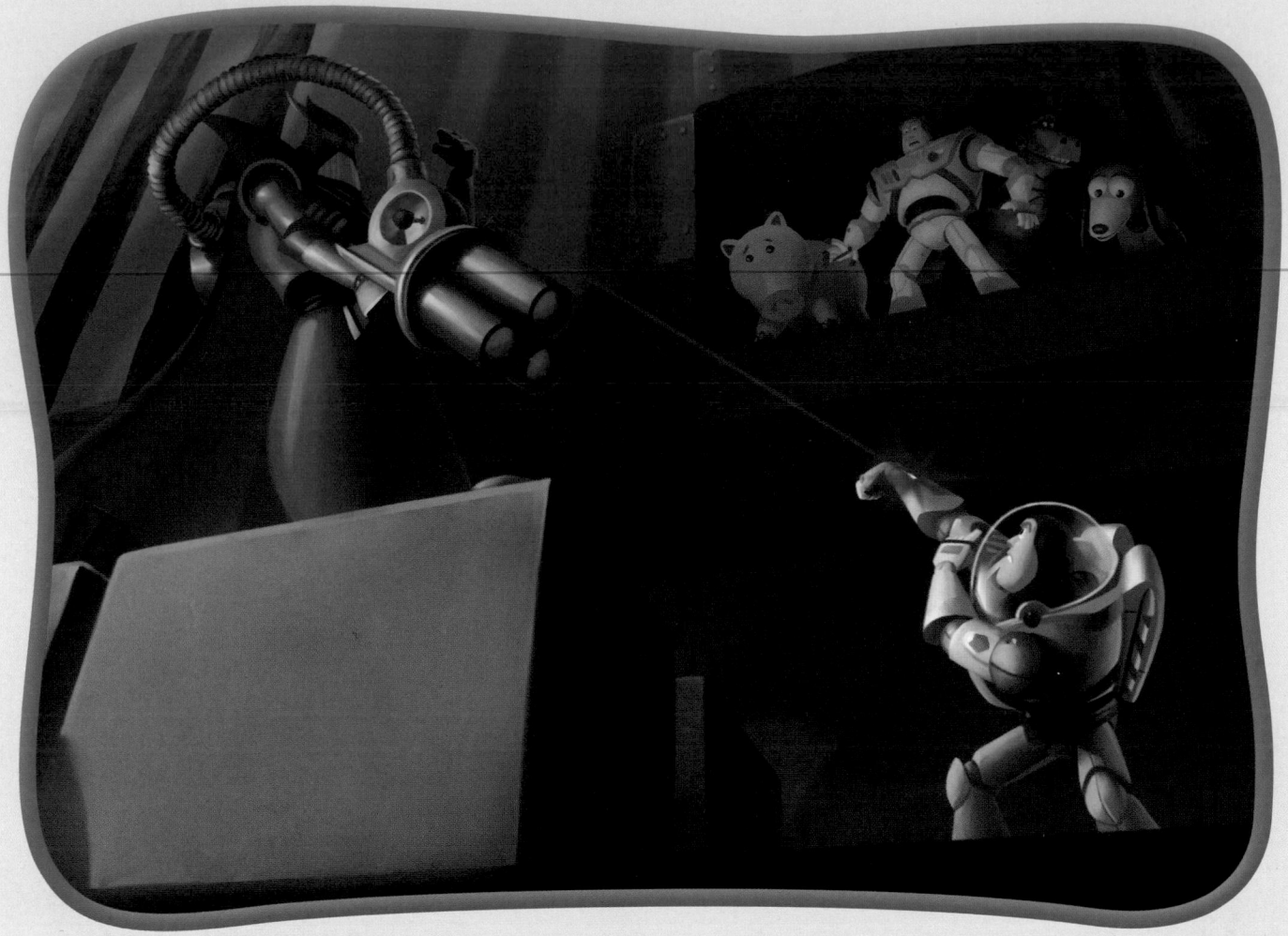

Al packed Woody and the other Roundup toys in a case and dashed out the door.

"We have to get Woody!" Buzz shouted. But as they headed for the elevator, they heard an evil laugh.

"It's Zurg!" gasped Rex.

Buzz and the new Buzz bravely fought off Zurg. Panicked, Rex closed his eyes and turned away. *Thwack!* His tail knocked Zurg over. Rex had defeated Zurg!

Al was getting away! Luckily, Mr. Potato Head spotted a pizza truck nearby. The toys jumped in and set off for the airport.

They found Al at the check-in desk. As his bag thumped onto the conveyor belt, the toys jumped on beside it.

Thousands of boxes, bags, and suitcases swept past them, but Buzz kept his eyes on Al's green case.

Buzz ran along the conveyor belt. Finally, he reached the case carrying Woody. But when he opened the bag, it was Prospector Pete who popped out. *Pow!* He hit Buzz.

Buzz fought back. Soon he had tied the Prospector to a passing backpack.

Meanwhile, Woody and Bullseye had managed to get out of Al's bag. But Jessie was still trapped inside!

Woody jumped onto the plane. He searched the bags until he found Jessie. "Come on, Jess," he said. "It's time to take you home."

Just then, the plane started to move. They had to get off!

Woody and Jessie found a hatch and crawled down to the plane's wheels. It was hard to stay on, and Woody slipped. Luckily, Jessie grabbed his arm just in time.

Woody's hat flew off, but it was caught—by Buzz! He and Bullseye were riding alongside the plane.

Woody looped his pull string around a bolt on the plane. Then, grabbing Jessie, he swung down under the plane and dropped onto Bullseye's back!

Woody smiled and looked at his friends. "Let's go home!" he said.

A few days later, Andy arrived home from cowboy camp. When he saw the new toys on his bed, he was thrilled. But he was even happier to see Woody! He couldn't wait to play with all his cowboy toys.

Woody and Jessie smiled at each other. They knew they were finally back where they belonged.